D0478568

INTERRUPTING CHICKEN
COOKIES FOR BREAKFAST

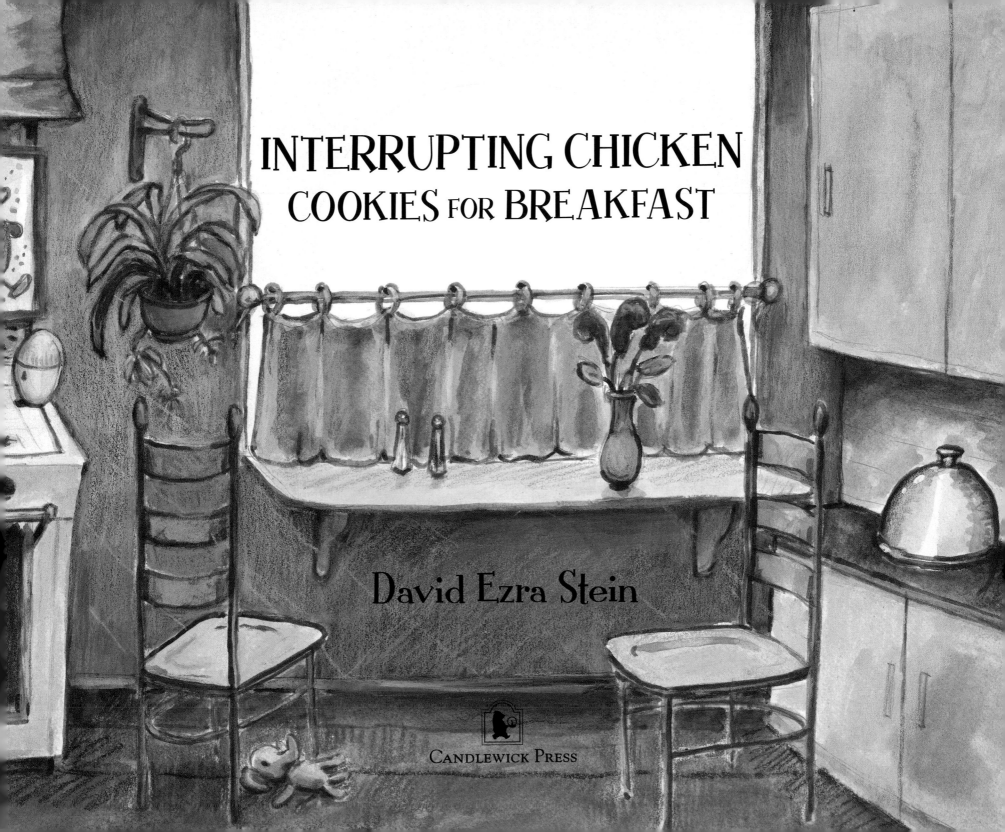

INTERRUPTING CHICKEN
COOKIES FOR BREAKFAST

David Ezra Stein

Candlewick Press

It was bright and early for the little red chicken.

"Good morning, Papa!" said the little red chicken.

"Oog," said Papa.

"Wake up!"

"Chickennn," groaned Papa, "I don't want to wake up yet. It's Saturday!"

"But look! I brought us breakfast in bed."

"Really?" said Papa.

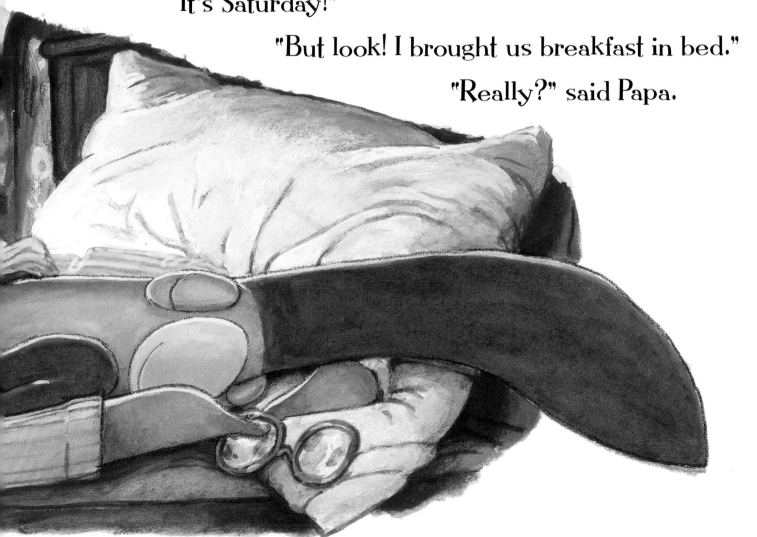

"Yes! It's cookies."

"Chicken, I don't want cookies for breakfast!"

"Then, can I have your cookies?"

"*You* are not having cookies, either!"

"Oh. Well, my *second* wish is to read a book with you."

"Okay," said Papa. "We can do *that*."

"Hooray! I'll go get a book!" said the little red chicken.

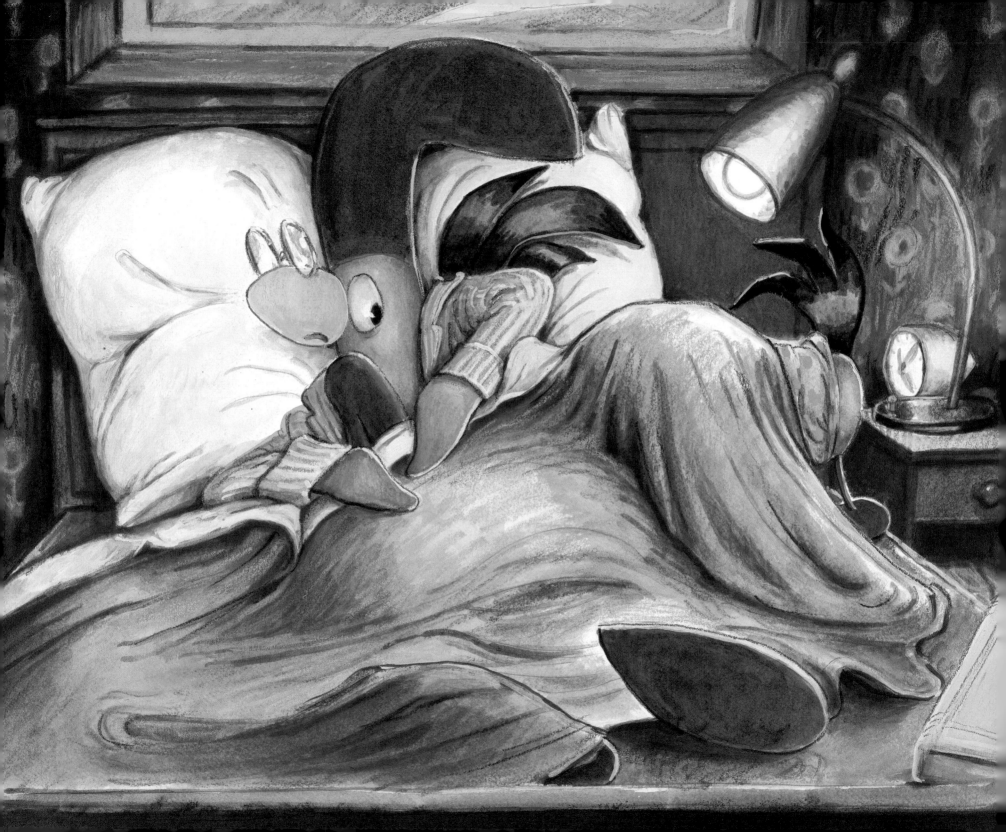

"Look out, Papa! Here I come! Ooh, it's so warm in the blankies."

"I know," said Papa.

"I brought nursery rhymes. I love nursery rhymes
because I love to rhyme: Papa be nimble, Papa be quick,
Papa read to your little chick."

"That's what I'm *planning* to do," said Papa.

"Well, don't let *me* stop you," said the little red chicken.

Diddle, Diddle, Dumpling

Diddle, diddle, dumpling, my son John
Went to bed with his stockings on;
One shoe off and one shoe on,
Diddle, diddle, dumpling, my son John.

There Was an Old Woman

There was an old woman
who lived in a shoe.
She had so many—

"Chicken."

"Yes, Papa?"

"We are not having cookies.
I'll make you a healthy breakfast as soon as I get up."

"Cookies are healthy! They have lots of vitamins."

"What vitamins?"

"Vitamin C, for cookie!"

"Let's just read, okay?"

"Okay, Papa."

Humpty Dumpty

Humpty Dumpty sat on a wall,
Humpty Dumpty had a great fall.
All the king's horses
And all the king's men
Couldn't put Humpty together again.

Jack Be Nimble

Jack be nimble,
Jack be quick,
Jack—

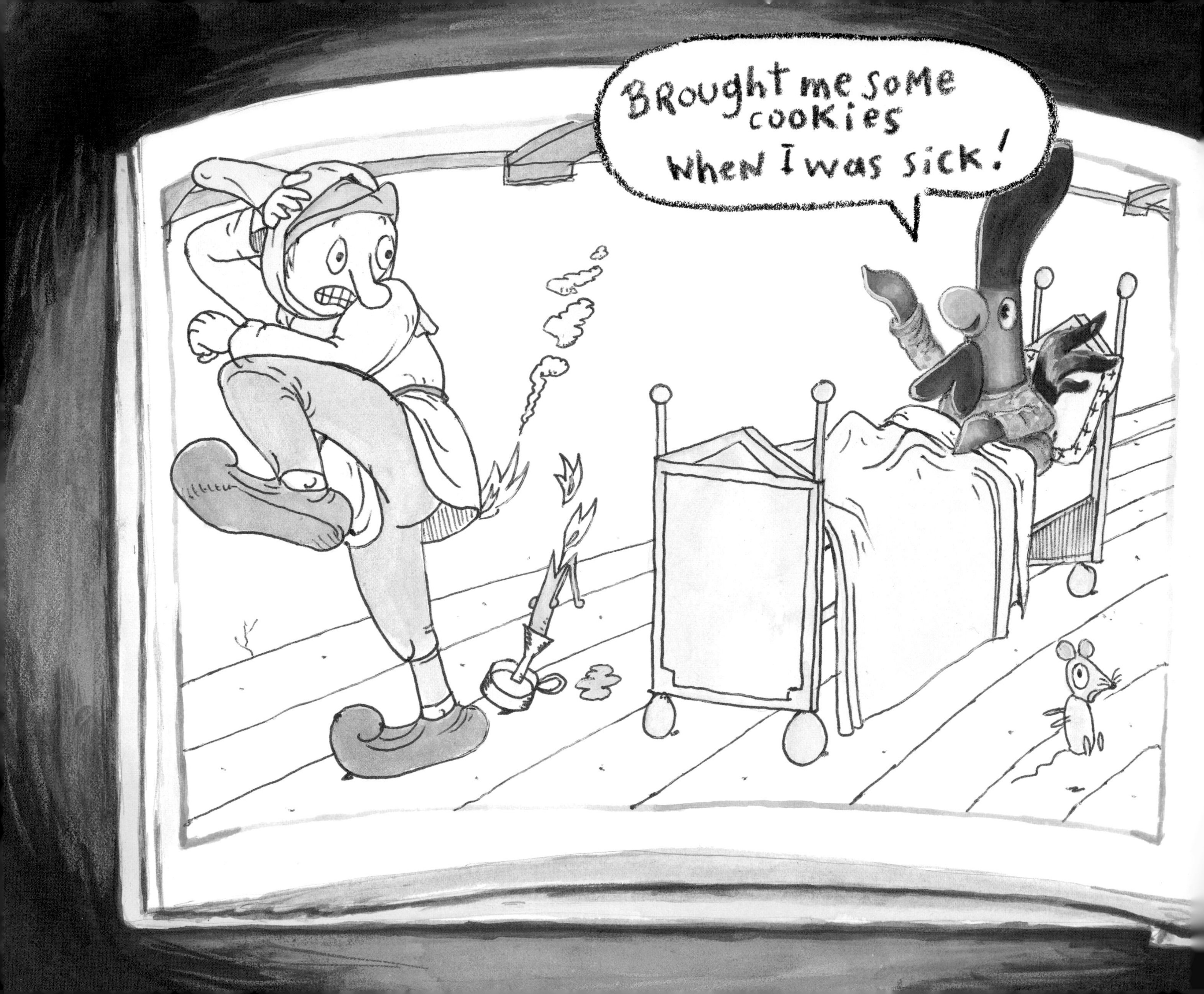
Brought me some cookies when I was sick!

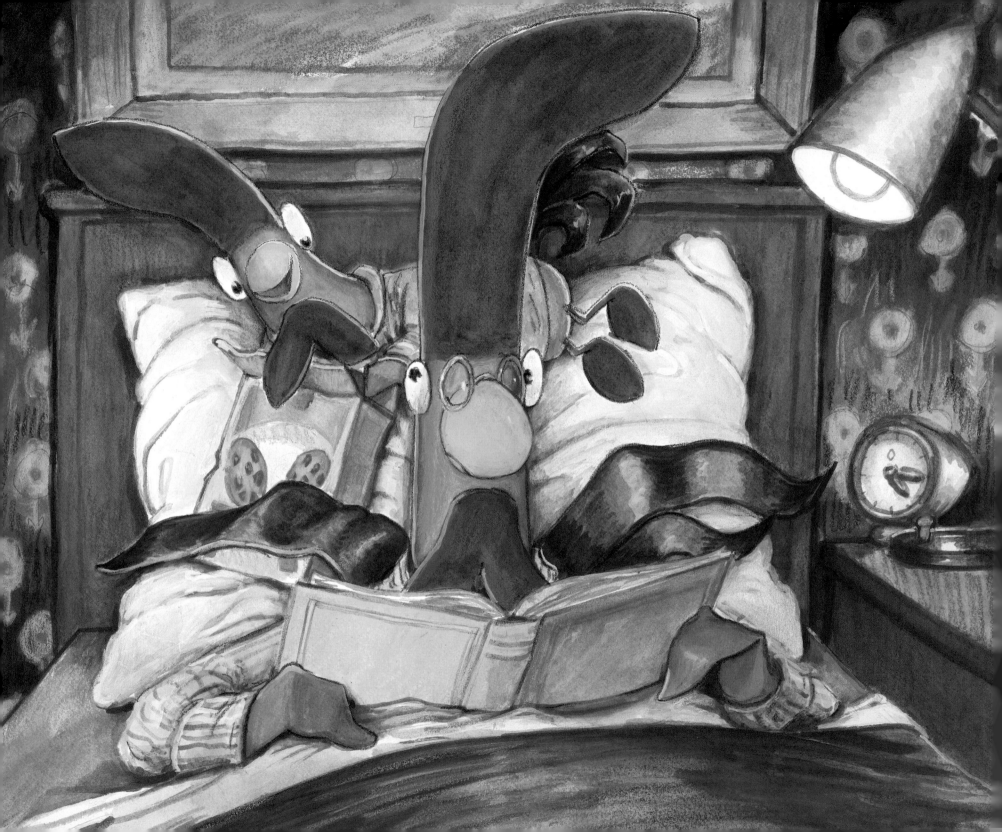

"Chicken."

"Yes, Papa?"

"I told you, we can't have cookies so early."

"I heard the early bird gets the cookie."

"That's *worm*."

"Well, you can have a worm, but I'd rather have a cookie!"

Papa yawned. "We'll have breakfast soon.
Let's just read a little longer."

"Okay!" said the little red chicken.

Little Boy Blue

Little Boy Blue,
Come blow your horn.
The sheep's in the meadow,
The cow's in the corn.

Where is the boy who
looks after the sheep?
He's under a haystack
fast asleep.

Hickory, Dickory, Dock.

Hickory, dickory, dock—

"Chicken."

"Yes, Papa?"

"Putting cookies into the nursery rhymes isn't going
to get you cookies for breakfast."

"How about cookies for lunch?"

"No. Cookies are only for dessert or snack!"

"Uh-oh. You see that, Papa?
The cookies got cold because we didn't eat them in time."

"Why were the cookies warm in the first place?" asked Papa.

"Because I sat on them. Nobody likes a cold breakfast, Papa."

"Okay, Chicken . . . I'm going to rest my eyes
for a few minutes. I think I have a headache."

"Papa, don't close your eyes! I'll be lonely."

"Aw. Come here, Chicken," said Papa.
"Snuggle under my wing."

"Okay, Papa! And I'll write you a nice loud poem—
    I mean a nice *relaxing* poem—while
        you rest."

                "Sounds good," murmured Papa.

"What was that, Papa? A bear? A lion?"

"No, Chicken. That was my stomach. I guess I'm hungry!"

"Does this mean we can have cookies for breakfast?"

"I have a better idea," said Papa. "We can have cakes!"

"We can't have *cakes* for breakfast, *can* we, Papa?"

"Yes," said Papa . . .

"pancakes."

To my niece, Lucy, one smart cookie

First edition 2021

Library of Congress Catalog Card Number pending
ISBN 978-1-5362-0778-1

21 22 23 24 25 26 CCP 10 9 8 7 6 5 4 3 2 1

Printed in Shenzhen, Guangdong, China

This book was typeset in Malonia Voigo.
The illustrations were done in watercolor, water-soluble crayon,
china marker, pen, opaque white ink, and tea.

Candlewick Press
99 Dover Street
Somerville, Massachusetts 02144

www.candlewick.com